The Muddy R

By Gregory March

Illustrations by Yae Yeung

The Muddy Road

Written and published by
Gregory March

www.tanzanandekido.com

Illustrations by Yae Yeung
www.facebook.com/yae.yeung

Edited by Nick Scott

Design by Lamma Studio Design

ISBN-13: 978-1515368045
ISBN-10: 1515368041

Tanzan and Ekido are friends of the very best kind. More like brothers, actually.

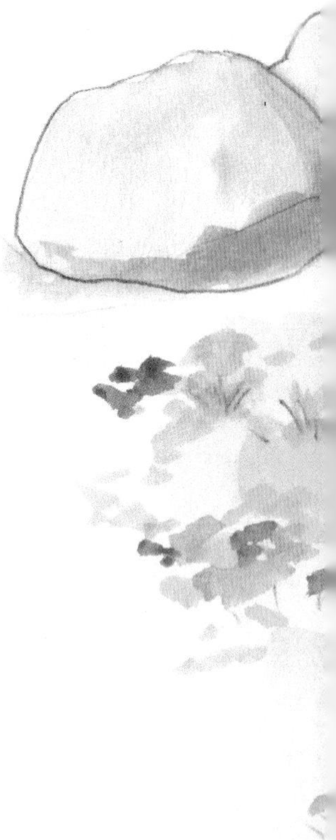

They play together but sometimes fight. They always make up and forgive one another, then look at each other and laugh.

This is the story of Tanzan and Ekido taking a walk on a muddy road in the rain. Tanzan is enjoying the puddles but Ekido is grumpy — and about to learn a lesson…

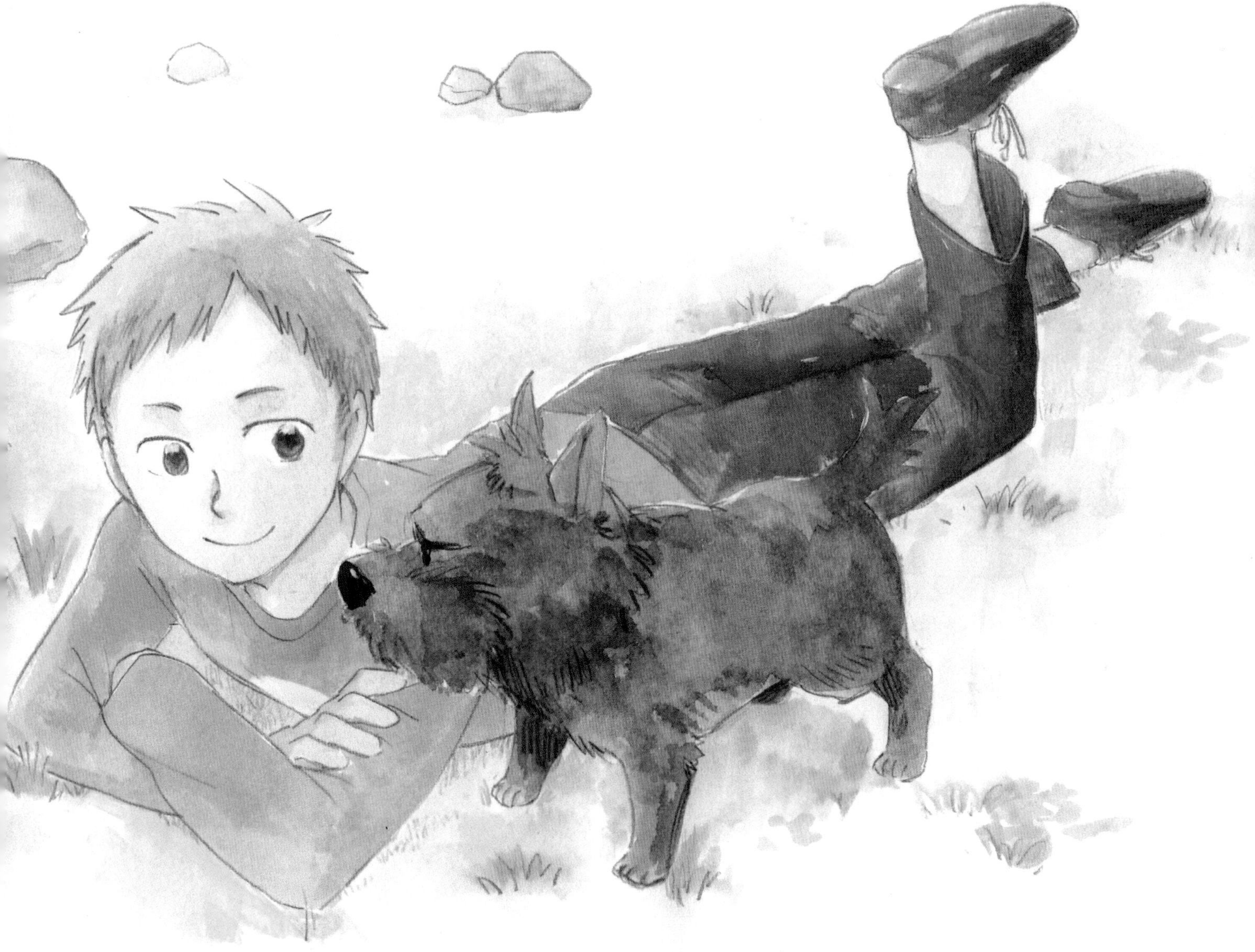

"Woo Hoo, it's raining," says Tanzan. "Let's go and jump in some puddles!"

Ekido doesn't want to get muddy but he goes along anyway.

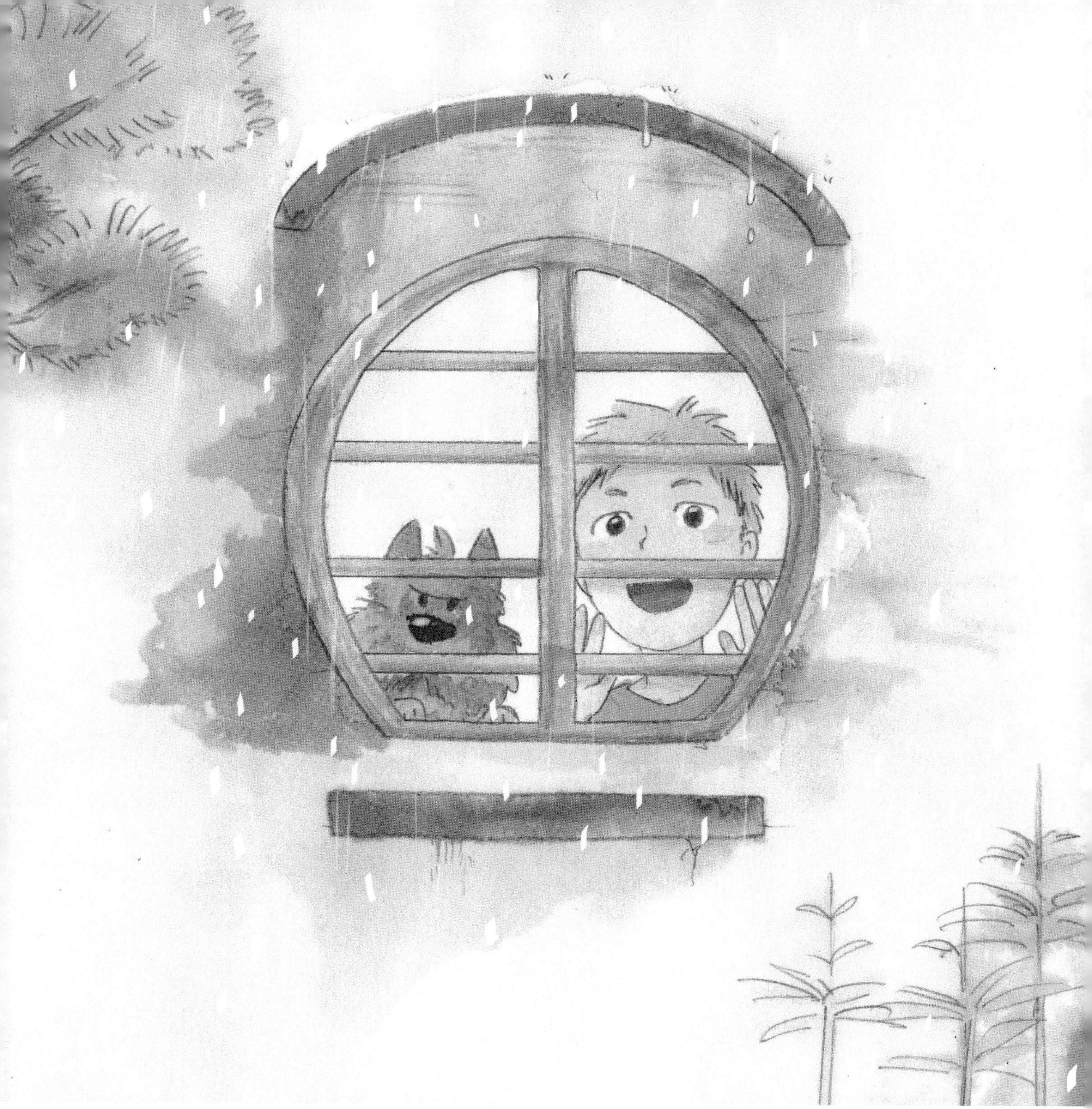

Tanzan jumps joyfully in muddy puddles in his wellington boots.

Ekido walks grumpily by the roadside.

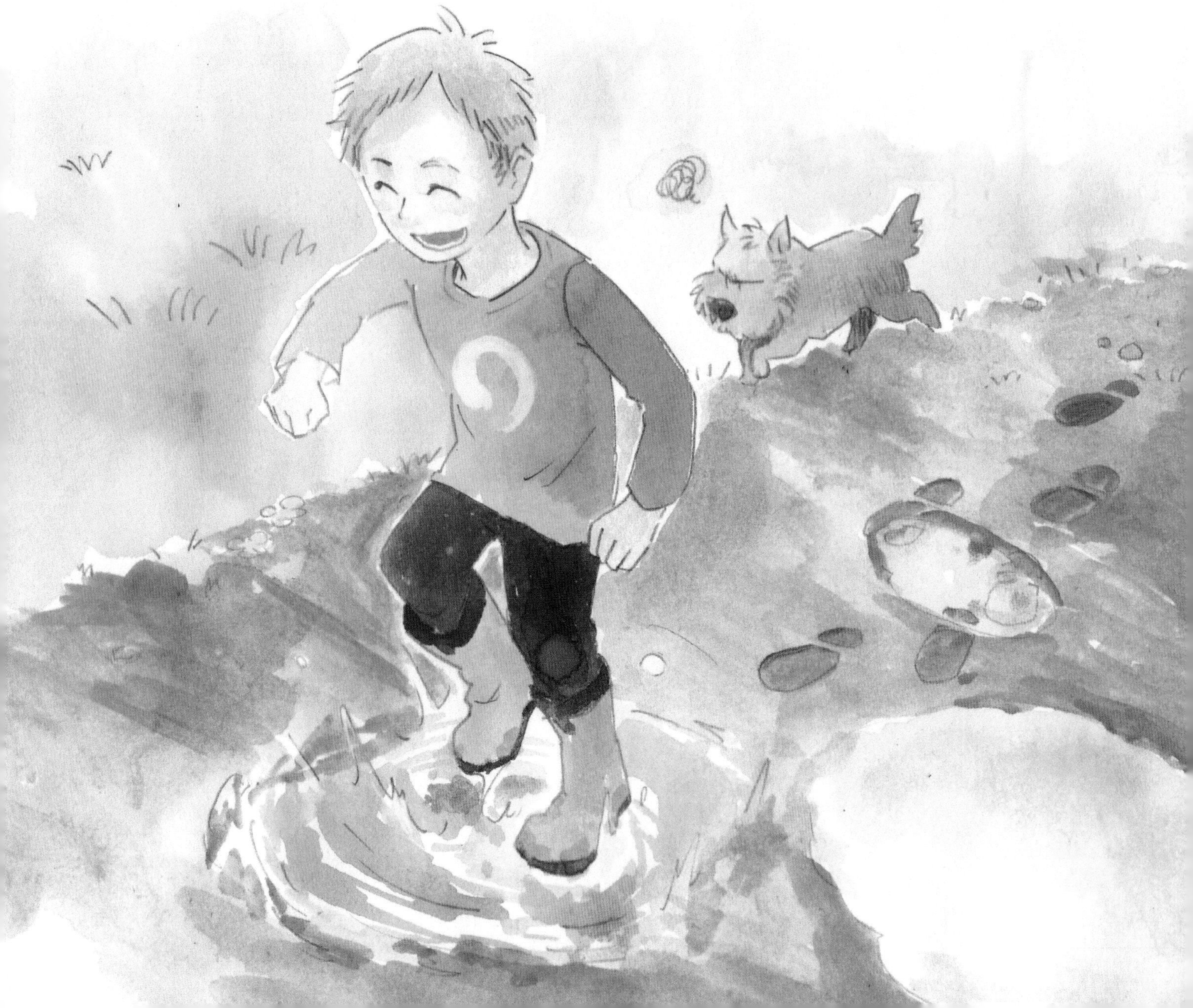

As Tanzan and Ekido come around a bend, they meet a lovely white dog in a beautiful red ribbon.

She cannot cross the muddy road.

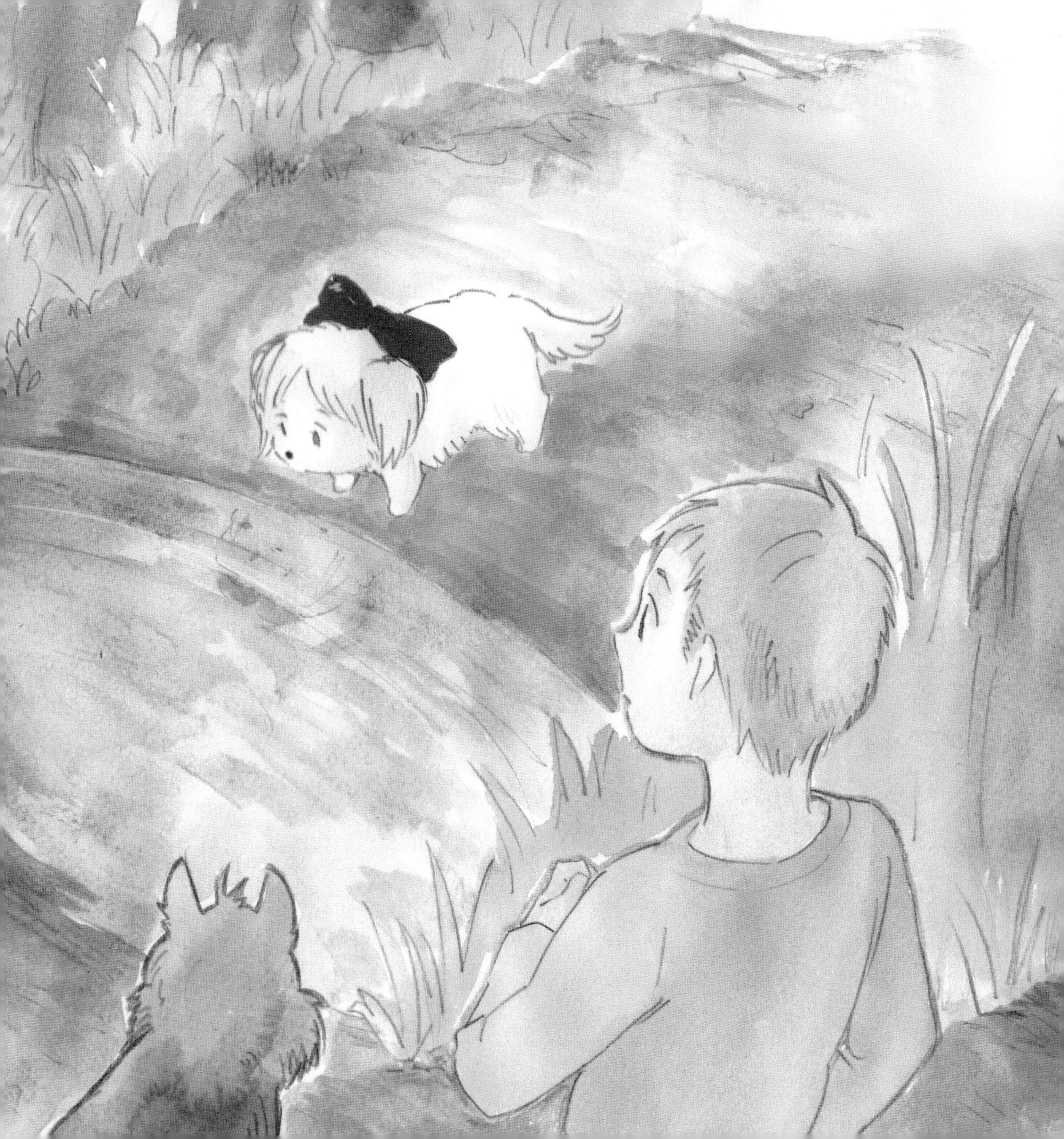

"Come on, girl," says Tanzan at once. He then picks her up and carries her across the muddy road.

Ekido is angry.

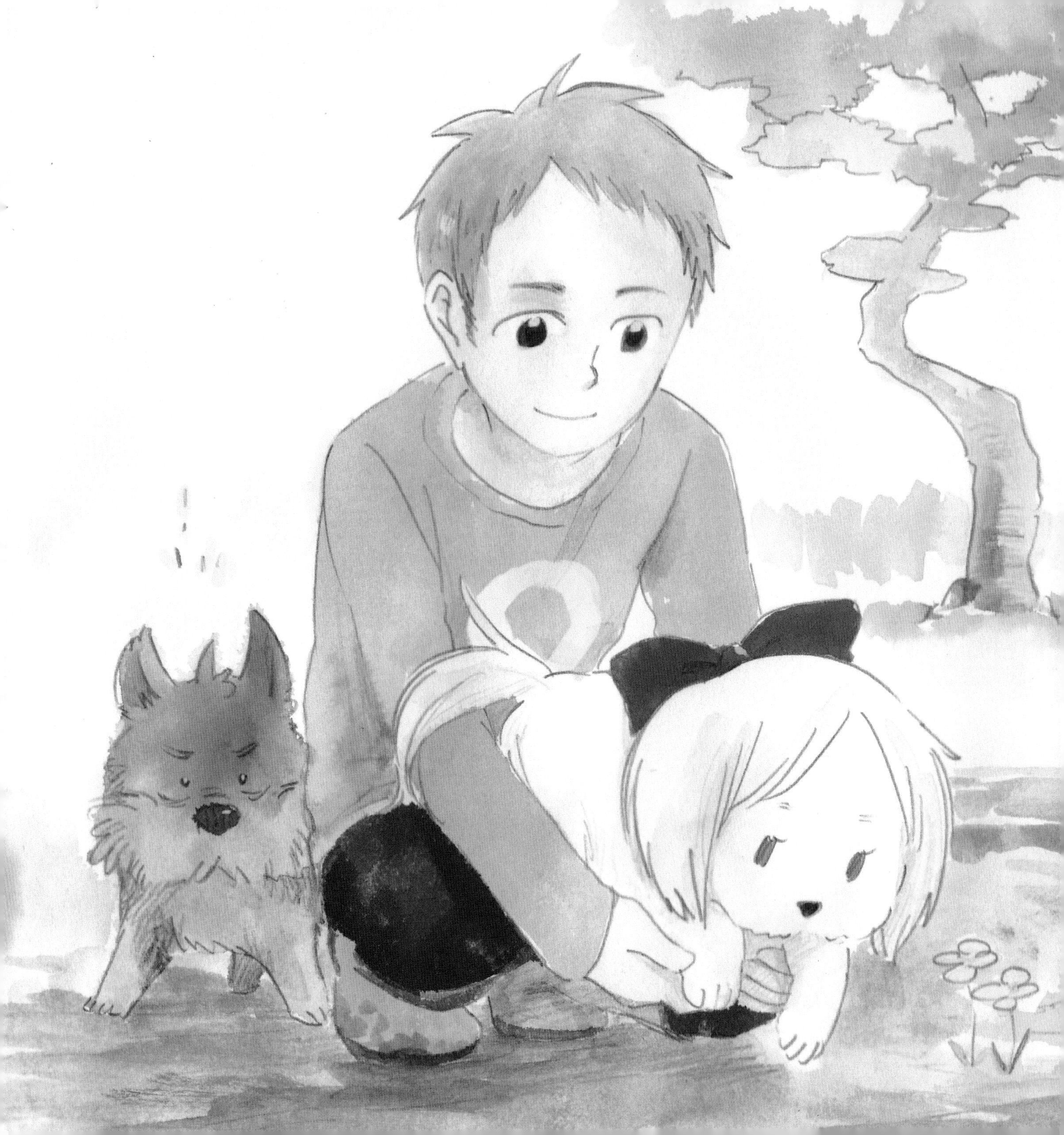

Ekido does not speak to Tanzan all the way home.

Tanzan enjoys more puddles and the smell of the wet earth after rain.

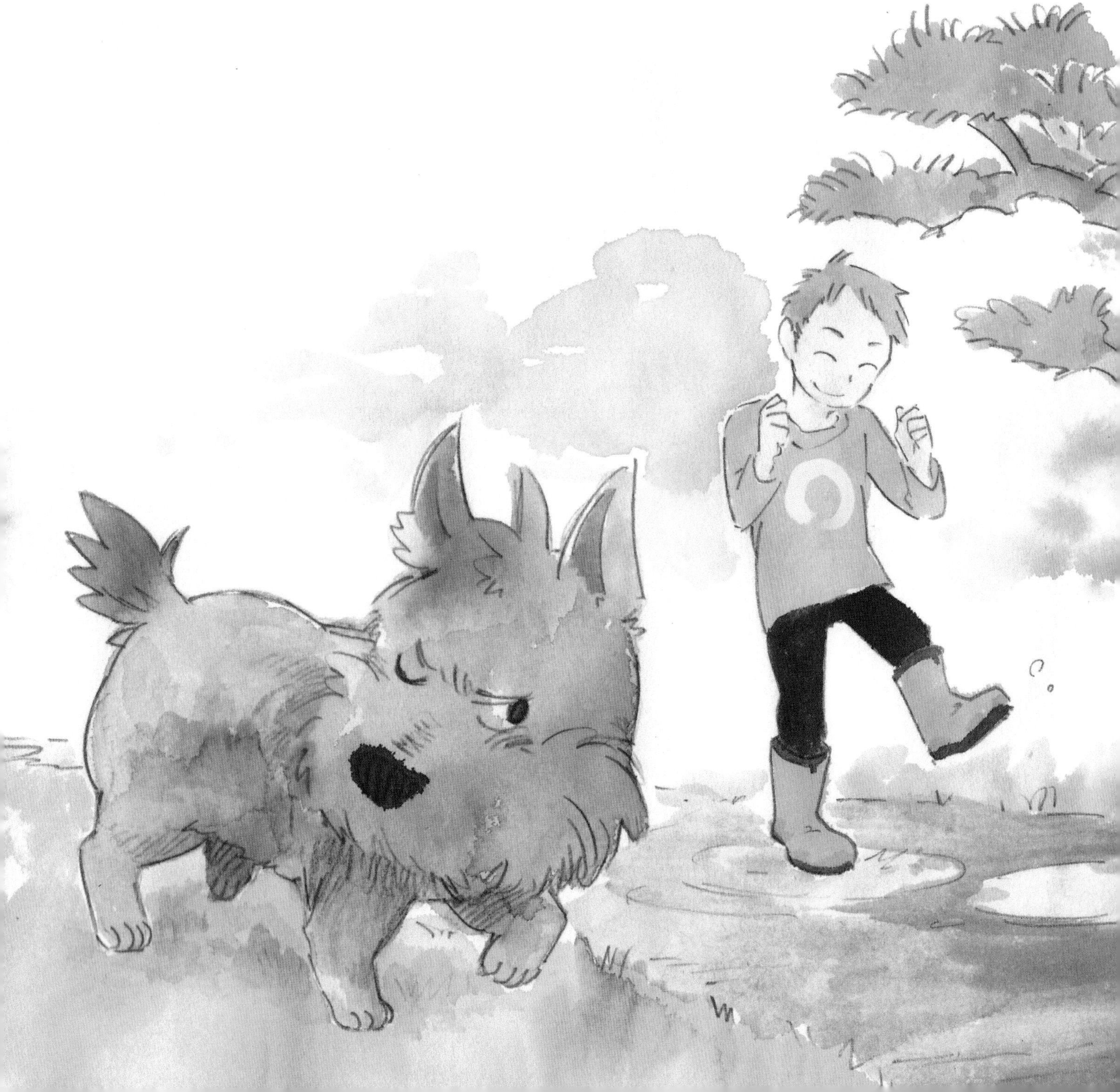

Later that evening, Ekido finally cannot take it any more.

"Why did you pick up that other dog?! You are MY friend! You are not supposed to do that!" Ekido growls.

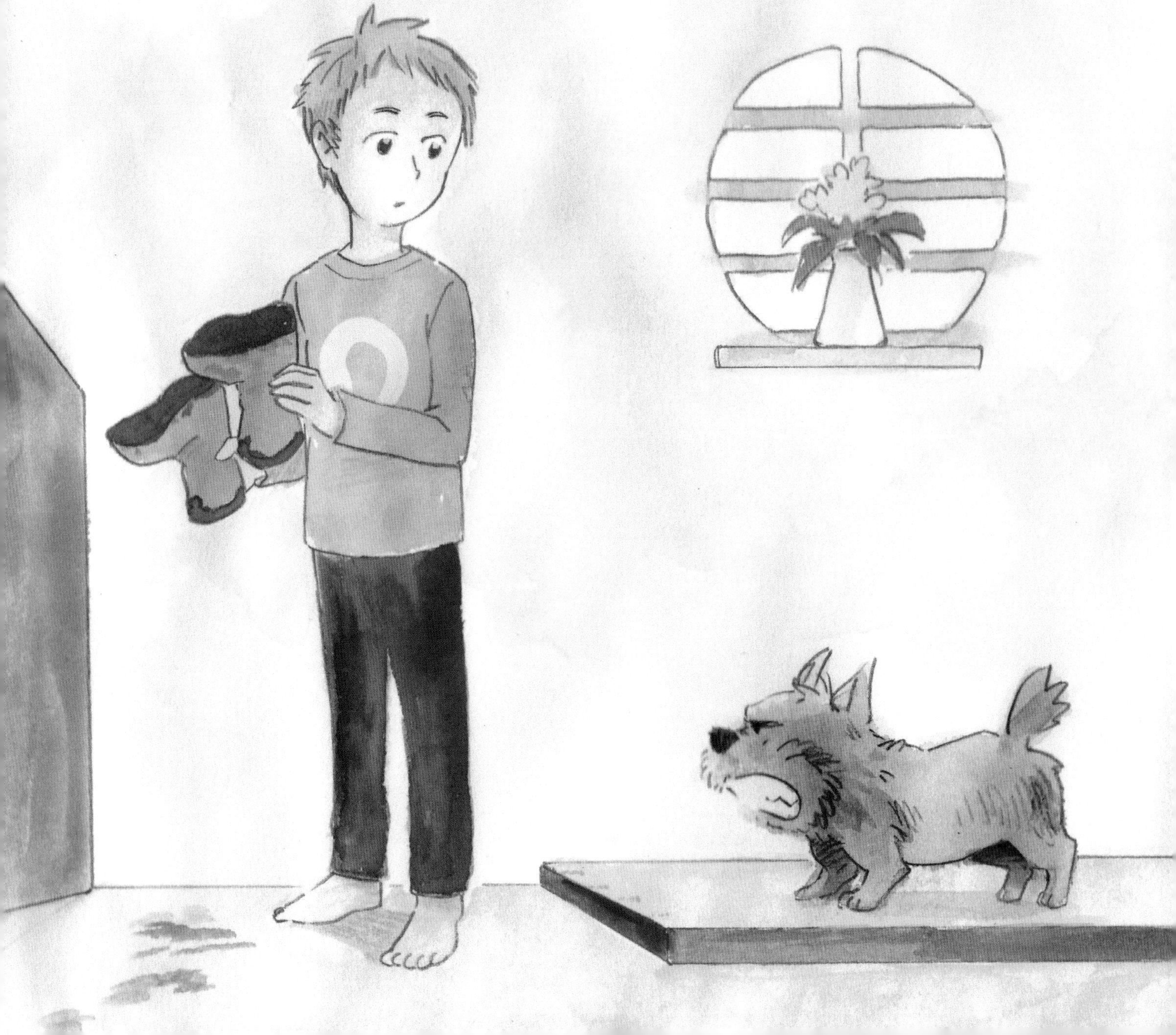

"I put her down there at the muddy road," says Tanzan. "Are you still carrying her?" Tanzan smiles.

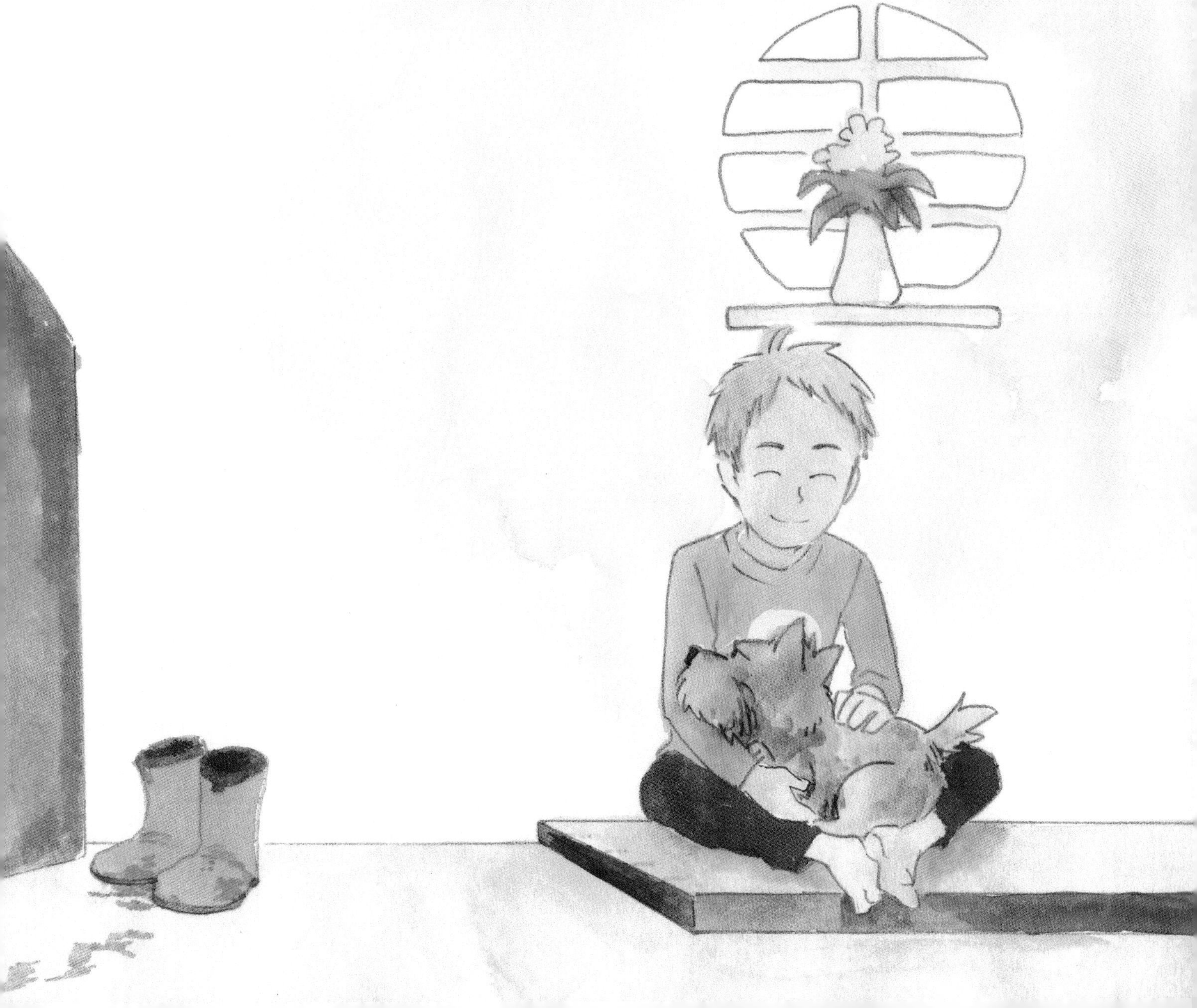

The End.

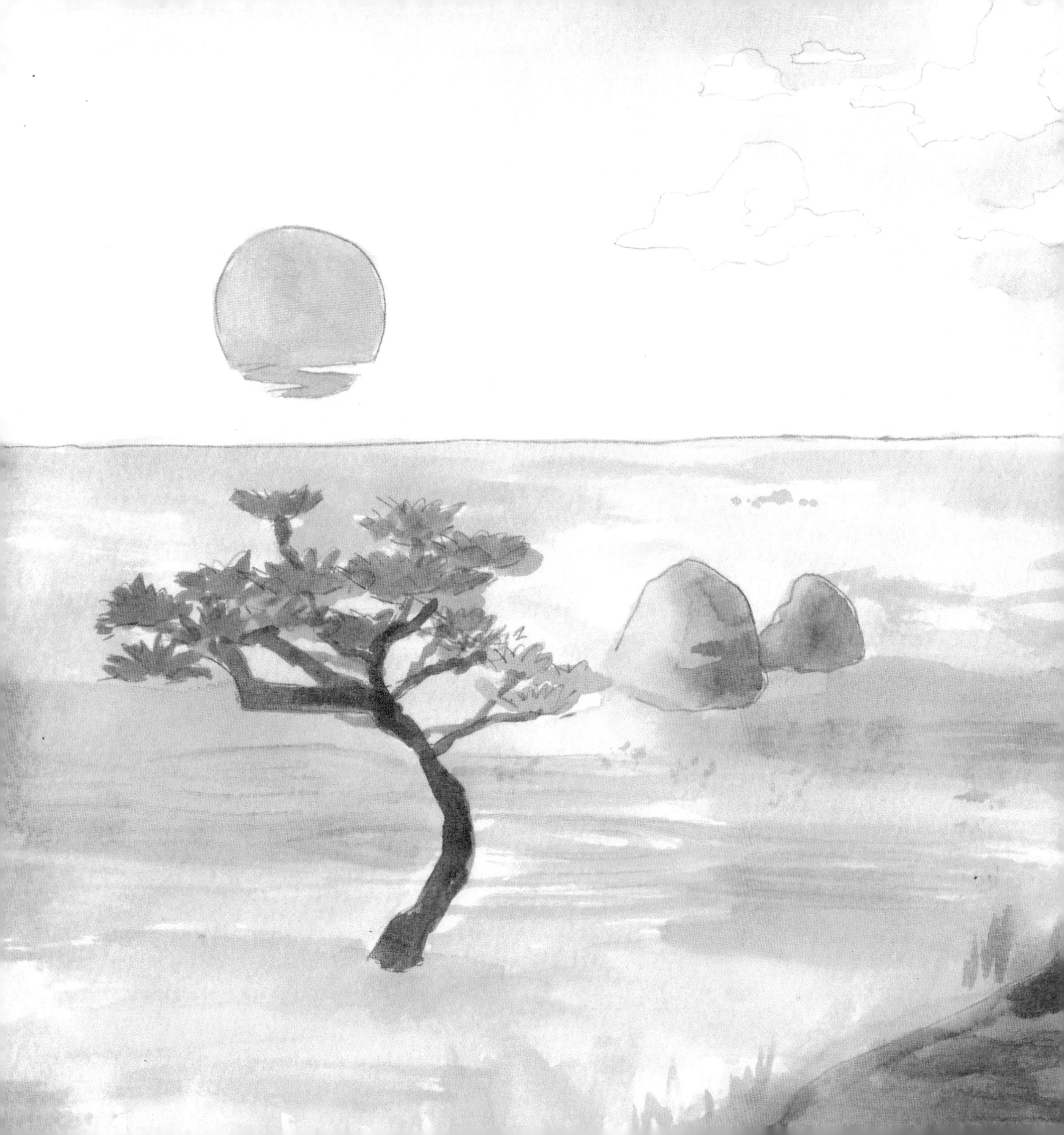

Gregory March

Greg lives on Lamma
Island, Hong Kong with
his beautiful wife Judy
and wonderful sons James
and Michael, who
inspired him to write this book. Greg has passionately enjoyed Zen
stories since childhood when his Dad gave him a book of them and
they often make him laugh.

Yae Yeung

Yae Yeung loves reading and drawing Manga (Japanese style comics). She studied in a manga school in Japan for 3 years and loves drawing the interactions between humans, living things and nature. Facebook: www.facebook.com/yae.yeung